The W

A Science Fi

C000130395

Many thanks to my family.

The Water Theft
A Science Fiction Short Story

Topaz Hauyn

Besuchen Sie uns im Internet:
Visit us online:
www.topazhauyn.de
www.topazhauyn.com

ISBN 9798587110335
Coverdesign Topaz Hauyn
Art innovari/depositphotos.com
Font Alegreya

Gravity was reinstalled on the ship. They had safely left Sowa and were now heading home.

Zelon looked down at the screens in front of him. Everything was alright. The water was safely stored in the tanks. They could leave Sowa now, flying back to their home planet. The route was calculated and the speed was adjusted to the extra weight and inertia added by their valuable cargo. The energy would be more than enough to bring them home to Xarthe. Zelon stretched his arms and moved his shoulders in circles to eliminate the tension from the travel so far. He felt much more relaxed now and his staff members slowly started to relax too.

He turned to the water dispenser and filled a glass for himself. The water looked like it always did. Crystal clear. He took the first sip. There was no taste on his tongue. It was clean and fresh water. No comparison to the rehashed water he drunk on his way to Sowa. The rehashed water always had a bitter taste and was somehow stale. Yet it fulfilled it's purpose, keeping them alive.

He finished his glass and looked around. Everyone waited for him to give the command.

"Let's go", Zelon said and the crew on the bridge started the engines for the long distance jump, which would bring them close to home. Soon Sowa was a little point on their star map, and they were on their way.

Zelon walked around the bridge inspecting the different terminals, his officers were monitoring, navigating or working on. A task he would have preferred to do from his place. But he couldn't read the reports on the captains console. Security reasons, had his father said, when Zelon had complained for the first time. His console was in its own network on the ship. Connected to the weapon system. Weapons he shouldn't have, given his spaceship was a transporter and an old one, although it was very reliable. He made do with the extra work despite the itching, too tight clothes that were full of mud from the water gathering.

Everyone one of his officers he passed signaled okay with a snap of their finger: Fuel, health environment on the ship, other observations, communications, and clear space ahead for the flight home. They could make the jump alright.

Back on his place, Zelon waited and observed the jump. Only a few more hours to fly home through space. Time for a little pause, he decided. This would give him the chance to change clothes and get rid of the mud and dust he was covered in from being on Sowa. He logged out of the captains console, waved his first officer Maurke on his place and turned to the door. A bit of reading and a refreshing syrup bread would be great after changing into comfortable Xarthian clothes. They had much more room to move, instead of those tight and stiff Sowan trousers and shirts.

Zelon was half way down the hall to his rooms, when he heard his first officers voice through the communication system: "Zelon, we need you on the bridge."

The voice of his first officer sounded anxious and Zelon furrowed his eyebrows. He hadn't even reached his room and was already called back? What could go wrong in a minute or two, he asked himself, but already turned around storming back to the bridge. His boots stomped on the floor and left little heaps of mud. The crew members in the hall quickly give place hearing and seeing him storming in their direction. Seconds later Zelon put his key on the reader screen and waited, walking back and forth on the spot, for the door to open.

Zelon stopped mid-movement, one foot still in the air.

The lights on the bridge had changed from light yellow to alarming dark green. On all screens he saw from his place was the image of his older sister Arlina. Did the gossipy news organizations run another search Arlina campaign, because she was beautiful and still not found, after years of searching? He bite his teeth. Couldn't they leave his family alone after so much time?

His staff members stood together in the middle of the room at his place, the captain's place, huddled together. They looked scared. Scared by a picture? Zelon wondered and put his foot on the floor, then walked on the bridge.

"What's up?", Zelon asked his staff. The room was silent. Nobody seemed to notice him.

"Arlina", Maurke pointed on the console in front of him. "She threatens to destroy our ship and offers to let us go when we surrender."

So she was back then. He had always expected her to show up again one day.

"She did what?"

Zelon walked over to the console pushing some people away.

"She also wants you as a hostage, Zelon", Maurke added, as Zelon stood next to him.

Zelon looked up. "What?"

Arlina was back? Healthy and alive? He stared at Maurke without really seeing him. How would she look like today? Surely she had grown older, hadn't she? Still the screens showed the last official image available off her.

He couldn't find more words. What did Arlina plan now? His older sister had vanished years ago, why would she need the water they bought for Xarthe? Why taking him hostage? Why hiding for years?

Knowing no answer to those questions, he turned to what he could really find out: "What else did she do? Why are you standing here instead of in front of your consoles?"

He looked into the faces around him. They all pointed down to the little picture at the bottom of the screen.

"Those are the remaining pieces of Xarthe", stood there.

Zelon enlarged the picture with a hand gesture. All he could see was empty space and some asteroids. A huge amount of dust. Like part of a nebula but much smaller, given the measurements at the side of the image, indicating it was more like an explosion of a small planet.

"Her work?"

Zelon looked at the picture, wondering how Arlina managed to destroy a full planet or had she just faked it like so many other things in her life? She was nearly perfect at faking things and that was her weak point: Nearly. She had been caught sooner or later. Always. Therefore he hadn't really believed she was dead. Gone, hidden, vanished, sure. But not dead.

"Just teaching you a lesson for stealing my spaceship command, little brother." Arlina's voice came from the loudspeakers on the bridge full of hatred and anger.

Zelon felt how his staff members stepped aside, making room around him like he was an infectious disease. He could understand them but felt very alone now. He wasn't responsible for his family members actions. The destroyed planet meant dead family members to him, too, he thought bitterly. His sweet, three-year old, daughter he would never cuddle again, and his beloved wife, both dead like millions of other Xarthian inhabitants.

He closed his eyes. The mission was useless from one second to the next. No one needed the water anymore. But he still needed fresh clothes. Another useless aim.

"I'm waiting, little brother", Arlina's voice was cold over the loudspeaker. "Will you surrender, hand me over the resources and yourself as a hostage?"

Zelon looked up and around. Why should he do so? Arlina would destroy the ship after she got what she wanted. He saw the same thoughts in the eyes and faces of his staff.

All of them would die.

"Zelon, she wouldn't let us live", Maurke said what everyone thought.

The laughing of Arlina was confirmation enough.

"Besides, where should we go? Our home is gone", Maurke added.

"You could work for me", Arlina offered with a sudden change of sound in her voice. "I'm always in need of cleaners." Her laughter echoed in the room.

"Tell me, Arlina", Zelon said, "why do you need the water? Shall we use it to clean your ship? Besides, I didn't steal your command. You vanished and the ship needed a new captain. Where have you been all those years? Why come back now and destroy our home planet?"

So many questions he wanted answers too, but primarily he needed time, time to decide what to do next. Time to close off his grieve about his family and his home world.

Zelon stepped forward to his console, logged in and opened the map around the ship. Where was Arlina's ship? There, directly in front of them. Should he try to destroy her first with a sudden attack, forgoing to aim the weapons first?

"Look, little brother, there are other planets too, to live on. Just water is generally lacking. You should feel honored to survive", said Arlina.

His sister was so arrogant, Zelon thought, no wonder her tricks were always uncovered. She loved to brag too much about them. The next planet to live on was out of the reach of her spaceship, although it was a newer model than his transporter. Xarthe was intact and the picture was a manipulation. At least he hoped so.

"Which planet had you chosen as your new home?"

Zelon hoped to keep Arlina talking while he selected the weapons from his menu. She hadn't reacted to his doings so far so it seemed as if she only used the voice transmission. He made a small sign for his first officer. Maurke nodded, then slowly moved toward the next console he could reach. Silently.

"A beauty, dear brother. One you'll like coming to. Besides, I saved your precious daughter and brought her there, before destroying our planet", said Arlina.

Zelon pressed his lips firmly together. She couldn't have kidnapped his daughter. She was heavily guarded, like his wife and their parents.

"Why did you leave in the first place?", asked Zelon.

He pressed a few more keys on his console. The dirty, tight clothes itched on his skin. But he forced himself to concentrate. Focus on his task at hand and keep his sister talking.

Out of the corner of his eyes he saw Maurke reaching the console and touching the surface to log in as first officer.

A clattering bang filled the bridge followed by noises of pain and a cloud of smoke raising from the console Maurke moved too.

Zelon smelled the stinking smoke and pressed the next button on his console hearing Maurke groan with pain.

The weapon slots opened and weapons were fired.

She did control the space ship!

Zelon turned around to see Maurke lying on the floor with the jacket of the weather engineer on his arm to extinguish the flames on his arm.

"Sorry", Zelon formed silently with his lips. Maurke nodded in silent acceptance.

"You won't use your consoles", Arlina commented the explosion. "I control them all. You have five minutes left, before I destroy the ship", she threatened.

She didn't mention his actions at the captains console. Couldn't she see them, as intended, or did she want him to feel save and cling to the last hope?

"I surrender", said Zelon. "Come over and collect me. Our transportation module needs fixing and I can't use it", he added hoping she would continue to oversee the mines he had set free. His unregistered mines he remembered. This would mean some inquiries back home. An inquire he looked forward to for the first time in his life, because that meant, the image of the destroyed planet really was a fake.

The moment Arlina materialized on his bridge, together with two of her staff members, Zelon pressed another button on the console and his security staff grabbed them. They arrested Arlina and her companion and dragged them off the bridge, down the hall. The mines exploded and destroyed her ship.

Relieved from the success messages on his console, Zelon motioned his communication officer to turn toward his console and contact Xarthe.

He waited. Like everyone else.

Down the hall he still heard his sister cursing and threatening him. He wouldn't answer. Others could question her and find out more about her plans and her schemes.

"Alive an healthy", said his communication officer.

Zelon sighed with relief, it had been one of Arlina's tricks.

He walked over to Maurke, who leaned against the wall, his arm already bandaged, ready to go to the medical room.

"You alright?", asked Zelon.

Maurke hung his head. "Lost the arm probably. But am alive."

Zelon hugged his first officer and friend. Then he called up the second officer to take over his place on the bridge.

Now he was going to change his clothes. He wanted to greet his daughter with clean clothes. And the investigator would be more willing to accept his explanations about unofficial mines if he looked fine.

Zelon left the bridge and walked down the hall towards his rooms. He opened the door with his identification card. The bride didn't call.

He waited a few more minutes, despite the itching and tightness of the clothes. But nothing happened. Relieved he undressed and stepped into the shower. The clean water they got from Sowa wasn't only in the storage rooms, but also in the ships water storage and he enjoyed every drop of fresh water running down his skin.

THE END

Excerpt

Served Like Red Wine

Someone had pushed the button to open the gray metal door from the outside. The shrieking sound of the mechanism pulling the door open hurt in Svenjas ears. Marry, the mechanic was informed. Just she happened to have no time this month. Therefore, Sveja would have to live with the noise. Or she had to close the café until the mechanic came around. If ever. The dishwasher in the kitchen behind her was still broken. A lack of spare parts to fix it the reason.

Used up, thick air blew into Svenjas face, coming in with the early and first guest of the day.

At least the air filtering was functioning, keeping the level of toxic gases in the air at bay. She didn't want to imagine the day the closing mechanism of the door would break and the door would be constantly open instead of just - shrieking each time used. Worse, the air filtering could break. Exposing her to the air outside in the streets with the much higher level of toxic gases.

A girl with white shirts, how the heck did she manage to keep them white with all the dirt, dust and the little water available?, stepped through the door. The heels of her shoes hit the floor like thunders of clashing clouds. A strange appearance here in the café at the center of the city. Behind her came into sight, in the bright light of the sun, heating up, the city center.

The girl walked straight up to the brown furniture table with the many scratches she had repurposed and used as the bar. Svenja saw the little wrinkles in the corners of the girls eyes. This was no girl. This was a woman who had seen life for at least three decades. Probably she even lived through the rough years where everything had broken down. The Earth's ecosystem went havoc and scientists had scrambled to invent the tech necessary for mankinds survival. They had succeeded, thinking about the air filtering technology. They had failed, thinking about the little number of a few million people still alive.

The door stood still open.

Svenja could only hope that it would work soon. She hadn't any spare money to pay the extra rates she would need to make Marry work overtime. Neither did she have any jewelry of her mothers left she could trade in.

The woman pulled air filtering mask from her nose and mouth and stored it in her, also white, handbag.

"Cherry juice, please. Served like red wine", said the woman.

Svenja needed a moment to process the order. The air coming in from outside already slowed her thinking down. She had to focus on the womens wrinkles.

Cherry juice wasn't a beverage usually ordered around her place. Her regulars drank beer, or at least what was called beer these days. A brown something mixed with artificial flavors and some microplastic that would give the crown the shape of white fumes people recognized from old memories and the faded pictures around the walls.

"Cherry juice. A moment, please", said Svenja.

The shrieking noise of the door filled the, otherwise empty room again. Finally, the door started to close. The humming sound of the air filtering helped Svenja to take a deep breath of relief.

The door still worked.

She searched the small boards along the wall until she found the Cherry juice. On the other side of the door to the kitchen stood the glasses. A wineglass of all things. She had only a few left and had placed them at the top to the safest place in the room.

Svenja stretched her arms, steadied herself with her free hand on a board and raised on tiptoe. Her shoes were soft enough from wear she could do that. Her fingertips reached the glass and she got it down.

The heels of the woman hit the floor behind her, as she walked to the blind windows, where the chairs stood.

Excerpt end of: Served Like Red Wine

More books

A spaceship. An artefact. A traitor.
Will Alexandra survive?

Alexandra Humboldt, pri-
viledged reality creatress,
enjoys the solitude of the
garden. Usually nobody
gets alone time in the
precious gardens of the
spaceship. Their only re-
al memory of Earth and
source of their fresh food.
Despite the peace around,
work problems creep back
into her mind.

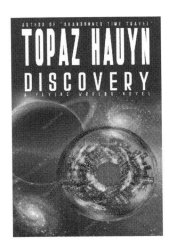

Alexandras job descripti-
on requires a vivid ima-
gination. A traitor turns
that upside down, and
steals the artefact needed
for the job and the survival of the space ship.

Discovery flies into an action-packed journey through
space and a fantastic way to visit new worlds.

Dive into the first novel of the new Science Fantasy
Series *Flying Worlds* by Topaz Hauyn.

Earth's ecosystem broke decades ago.
Svenja fights for survival, keeping her little café afloat.

Svenja repurposed trash to open her little café in city with a dwindling population. The air filtering and the door closing mechanism against the toxic air outside need repairs.

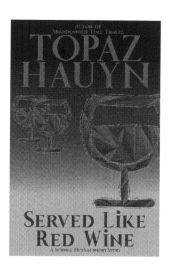

An uncommen visitor enters. Svenja estimates the woman at least lived through three decades. Including those rough years when Earth's ecosystem broke down. Something about the visitor says danger. Yet, she needs the money of every single guest.

A fast-paced near future fantasy short story about a bartender making ends meet.

Gabriella faces a tough decision.
The cold around her hinders thinking clearly.

Gabriella, responsible for communicaiton on the space vessle M41, rereads the declaration of war. The translation contains too many typos. No surprise, given the malfunctioning heating system. Gabriella freezes. The enemy outside does not answer. The protocoll must be fulfilled. Gabriella mistrusts the whole situation. She lived through a similar situation in this very area of space once. A false identification which killed people.

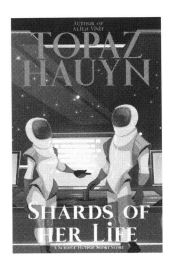

Shards of her Life combines politics, social unrest and the basic freedoms in a compelling story.

Daily life and security or alien item and curiosity?

Nea lives in the rainforest. Large leaves cover her from nightly rain.
A hard blue, foreign chip smashed through them. Nea never saw such an item.
Nea's curiosity rise. Who made this? Shall she find out and leave the security of her group?

In *Support Refused* an alien artefact smash through the peace of daily life in the rainforest.

Chocolate money, travel money, credit payments.
What could be more important?

Ramona fears the loos of her space ship. The tool she uses to earn a living. She bought it on credit. Her partner spent his Christmas salary on sweets. Money meant to pay the next credit rate. More than she knows depends on a fair solution.

Sweet Depths: Will Ramona find the balance between saving and spending?

In this galaxy-spanning universe money still dictates daily life.